Bullet Land
A book of poetry

by

Rajeshwar Prasad

TSL Publications

First published in Great Britain in 2024
By TSL Publications, Rickmansworth

Copyright © 2024 Rajeshwar Prasad

ISBN: 978-1-917426-04-6

Cover courtesy of:
https://pixabay.com/illustrations/floating-
islands-clouds-trees-5646926/

Dedication

For Bhagwati, my creator

O Goddess! You grew me up;
O Goddess! You loved me enough
And taught me to spread light.
Now you're in heaven – far away!

Contents

Bullet Land

A vision of chaos,
A madman reshapes the world,
With a chest broad as ninety-nine inches,
Hands of nineteen, feet of twelve,
To bring the bullet land to life;

Disordering all – God, scripture, society,
Politics, law, medicine, family, transport.

God replaced by the devil,
People worship bullets, desiring freedom,
Sex offered as thrill instead of holy gifts,
Fairies abound, youth are trenches birthing bullet men.
Sex is the scripture, endless bliss,
Sex, drugs and condoms for chaste appearances,
Never distressed, always fresh.

The bullet's message: decay, lust, greed,
Every evil under the sky thrives,
Wrong replaces right,
Sex and slaughter from bullet treasure,
Equality in perverse acts,
Eating flesh, blood, human infants,
Pleasure in the perverse is celebrated.
Saints in castles, better than leaders,
Enjoying fairies, condoms over scriptures,
Teaching deceit, banning essentials,
Free arms trade, arts by scientists,
Policemen as extortionists,
Men without culture, animals clothed,
Naked men lust for blood.

Foolish democracy,
Criminals in power, the virtuous punished,
Ten million laws for a few,
Virtuous beaten, the worst honoured,
Religion banned, evil thrives,
Clean roads for robbers, thorns for passersby.

Politics of division,
Activists killed, criminals praised,
Leaders of evil waging wars,
Bullet doctors, bullet hospitals,
Sex, drugs rewarded, sexual acts medalled,
Wives and husbands free from marital fidelity,
Punished for failing public lust.
Trains faster than thought,
Hundreds crash yearly,

Life taxed a thousandfold,
Weeping, laughing, everything taxed,
Except sex acts.

Praising the devil, seeking his boon,
Hate, unrest, violence, flaw, intolerance,
Bowing to the devil's power,
Seeking dark powers,
Ending light, sealing knowledge,
The devil's dominion over peace, love, truth.

A Letter to Lover

I love you, darling, really I love you
And I will pay for everything due.
I am here in a net of chivalry,
And society governs me completely.
I will be free from this atrocity –
I will thumb my all in-laws on duty.
I have married him as my parents willed,
In any way, and not because I loved.
I have not let him even touch my cheeks,
A thing of fun, touching my sex organs.
I'll live with you, not with any other.
Be sure, I am one, not as others are.
I am the same one, who has made you cool,
And you are the same, who have made me full.
I remember you even in night's dream;
My husband always tries to anoint cream.
He will get nothing except to see my face
In double veils of sari of his grace.
My sex organs are ever a dream for him.
Tomorrow, I'll be at my mother's home,
Where I will enjoy your high-voltage sex,
And you'll enjoy the pleasure of climax.
Yes, I have come here in search of your grace
I for meeting you in a lodge in a new dress,
Where you used to meet me for the sex race.
Aha! The Flora Hotel which used to give us peace
And pleasure lifelong, and never to miss.
Please surely reach there at nine in the morning
With the maximum sex force to ring
Taking a pellet and turning a rod
To satisfy me fully as you can,
As I am hungry, so fulfil your turn.

I have come here; bravo, you have also come.
Thank you take all this which is due to hum.
Please turn me cold as now I am too hot
And you must do all without a dot.

Aha! My darling, thank you, you have done well
Sucking hot liquid and getting me cool.
Now only one important task for you
Which I want to say, is fully now due;
That my husband has to come to meet me;
This is the proper chance, not let him see.
Otherwise, I have to face his motion;
I understand your fashion and passion.
You must do this chief task to take him out;
Coming to my own home, strangle his throat,
That will award immortal love to us.
Otherwise, we'll fail to fulfil our aims –
To let us continue our journey of love.
You are agreeing, so not work for me.
He has come here, but on his face, no glee.

My parents too agree to do the work
With a strategy to protect from the task.
After strangling, carry to the hospital
For admitting him, saying he is ill;
And mentioning the name of his father
As his guardian for treatment, later.
But bring nothing here – neither knife nor string
Because now we have managed everything.
Come soon! Have you come here? He is sitting.
Who is demanding water for drinking?
But nothing to him and his life in a fuss.
He's feeling all this and is afraid of us,
Willing to escape from here anyway.
But don't worry he can't save himself –
Neither will he enjoy the charms of an elf
Because all the rooms are closed outwardly.
Windows too, to not let the voice go out,
And now he will lose his life without a doubt.
Even God will not come to save his life
As I have already bought an edgy knife.
Aha! He is crying loudly, "Save, save, save.
They will kill me – my wife will kill me now –
My in-laws will kill me just like a cow.
They've closed me, so unable to escape…"

Okay! You have come now, go to the room,
And strangle him as soon as you can gloom.
Now my parents are ready to help you
I am also with you to fulfil what's due.
Take my long and strong kerchief to strangle.
Aha! All's well, thank you as you enable.
Now we will live in peace and pleasurable realm.
Take him to the hospital to save him from blame.
Yes, he's in the hospital where the name
Of his father to bother is given.
A case against his parents for his slain
With also a point of maintenance claim,
So no one will know our what deeds which we did
And we will continue to meet in need.

Only one year has passed since I suffer,
And you begin to forget your offer.
I am now suffering from breast cancer,
And advised to cut it by a doctor.
Take me to the doctor for an operation.
Why not? You enjoyed before my hymen
And when I was fully hot with liquid
Of teenage and made my organs lead.
Tell me, now what is wrong in doing so –
Why are you not fulfilling your old vow?
Who will expend money on my treatment?
I'm losing beauty, not my spirit.
Aha! If my husband were now with me here,
I would have faced my all woes this with dare!
Alas! You'll go away leaving me alone.
Fully using my body as a plaything;
Making my inner and outer as a ring;
And turning my sex organ into a drum;
Getting loss of losing one breast you are not warm;
Saying that I'm a woman without charm
You're only to enjoy my beauty –
And now why not fulfil your duty?

"O God! Excuse me for the sins, I have done
Neglecting everything only for fun.
Now all of my past deeds have been returned
And my love, peace, and pleasure have been burned.
I've only to enjoy sins in the arrears,
As my darling husband is not to bear."

Now Forever

"No one except you, indeed, whom I love;
And seeing you, my feet begin to move."
"I'm also in the same vein and too full.
So God has sent you here to get me cool.
On the drizzling night, full of sex and passion –
Too hot, I keep ice to check notion"
Kissing and embracing he moves his hands –
One towards both breasts and body bounds;
And another further down.
Following his loving moves she's to adjoin.
"We will dwell in pleasure without any rest."
"All the past records of love, we will bust."

They marry, are won by bodily bliss;
Beauty decreased, not the same kiss.
Family strife in place of enjoyment;
Promises forgotten, and no settlement;
Amid cloudy times, she becomes pregnant
But aborts as he beats in instalment –
In the seventh month instead of the ninth, at home.
The cases against in-laws, in a new realm;
They're arrested and detained in jail,
Where all enjoy the pleasure of hell.
Some get them compromised for their best.
But family strife is not to let them rest.

She, once again, gave birth after years;
Amid this, she talks over the phone to lovers.
He sees her red-handed and with too many beats.
Going to a hospital where she delivers.
The world media say "a child of strife",
Because it has tried to snatch her life.
Thus, in-laws are in jail and have no chance of bail;
Zero on reconciliation to dwell.

In so many cases, several times' jail march;
Living separately, sorrows they watch.
Several attempts for their compromise;

But not in a condition to gain a such prize.
Moving to spiritualism, even;
"Now in Light, now forever, for heaven."
"I wish you within me while closing my eyes
With new and ever-blessed immortal ties."

Sum Not Again

I discover the way which is unknown
By any other of this large world to date
Doing my miracles for gain, not vain;
Using new techniques to participate.
I'm one, who has qualified to take sum;
Otherwise, service is meaningless.
I'll place bogus bills and vouchers show'ng wisdom,
Turning the business of bribery into trades.
All the aims of my family I will grace
Without any stoppage for the great shower
Of rupees for heavenly pleasure and peace –
To develop my kith and kin faster.
My all predecessors will remain well
By the way, I only discover;
And enabling them all never to fall;
Even the top court cannot show anger.
If God awards me any golden chance,
My wealth will glow in the headquarter,
Where I will enjoy a modern grace
With costly clothes and new charms forever.
My house in town is better for a night stay –
Also for hoarding black money for safe;
For remaining away in any way;
And for consuming nectar in the cafe.
I have now a marvellous motorcar
For showing the high class to shine.
A dozen vehicles in future
For moving with fairies in red wine.
My palace is situated on the main routes,
From where I gaze at the crossroads –
With a huge check-point to my salutes –
And a temple of the deity for prayers.

I'll buy a house in the new capital –
For changing winter into spring fully –
For drink'ng wine with whores to good feel,
Where I will dance and sing gladly.

In five years of gazetted service –
I am able to handle such a way –
Fulfilling my deeds, but not in cut-piece –
Turning all this into routine of the day.
O God! Award me every golden chance;
And bless me ever for qualifying –
For only enjoying money glance –
For reaching Mars, and ever gaining.
Now I wish to go to the film stars' city –
For buying a huge shining bungalow –
Possible through the blessing of deity –
Where I will ever easily smile and glow.
Now I have black money in millions
To settle all this in a new city,
Where no policemen can trace my plans,
Where I arrange a banquet for pity.
God helps and blesses me forever gain;
And this golden chance I get from the divine,
So I, with my nature, never bargain;
Grotesquely, now none is in my line.
It's better to buy a house in the south,
To pass peaceful life on a rainy day –
For enjoying pleasure from the heart to mouth,
Where none will be able to send in clay.
Now, most of my good desires are complete,
And my all-black deeds are completely veiled.
None can consider – what I do and eat
As I'm an artist for doing such deed.

Aha! I'm fully satisfied with all things
Which I have arranged and which I consume.
Alas! The government knows all my black deeds
And has detained me in jail making me lame.
The court found me guilty of a crime
Which I had committed for illegal money.
Living in the central jail, I pass the time
Where no one is allowed to give whiskey.
The award of ten years' imprisonment,
And there is no chance of betterment.

Now slabs instead of cushioned beds in fate,
For which I say, but none wills to rebate.
Enjoying the tune of sins, I have done
Ignoring all virtues for black money;
Now no loving one comes and all has gone,
And all, of my office, consume honey.

O God! Enlighten mankind of the race
To turn activities into a boon!
O God! I am on sods and pine for your grace,
So now award me peace, not sum again.

The Godman

There was a monastery of millions
Spread over several hectares of land
With an underground makeup in the cave
Which was three-storeyed and heavenly too,
In which the millennium man lived;
Who declared him a godman?
Thousands of arms, and armed men with him
Godman for his protection in the cave –
His long white beard hung to his waist;
And his long hair fell below his thigh;
The sandalwood paste on his lucky forehead;
And shone the mark as the divine angel.

He chanted the lesson on charity;
A sex-addicted and evil deity
Whose bed cell was attached to she-saints.
He called all one by one in need
And so was a modern saint indeed.

He used to rape some of his she-saints,
And the case was filed for his arrest.
Devotees did not allow doing so.
He was arrested after taking toils,
His devotees wasted the property
Of millions for which he was fined.
He's found guilty and sentenced to jail
Where he is enjoying the charms of hell.

The Saviour

The temple of Tanot Mata in Jaisalmer –
Ten kilometres away from Pakistan –
And the hot year of nineteen sixty-five –
The war between India and Pakistan –
Starting, India was in a weak condition;
An attack of three thousand bombs on it,
Where many Indian armies took shelter
To save a life in that critical condition.
But all the bombs dropped targeting it,
Which came under the temple campus;
Not even one exploded within it.
But the same out of the campus exploded.

Once again in nineteen seventy-one;
The same shameful attempt of Pakistan;
When again all Pakistani tanks were stuck
Losing the lives of two hundred tank troops,
But then, not even a single Indian.
Pakistan's request to see Her miracle,
Which is granted by India, so arrived.
The officer was surprised to see it.
Paying respect, "This is a Goddess' miracle."
Presently, there're about three thousand bombs
Placed in the temple for worship;
And the temple under the Indian Force;
The place of miracles, faith, and tourism;
The holy place where physics fully fails,
And where firm faith in God ever remains.

The Ocean of Faith

A great man of great fate and great income –
Who possesses everything of the age –
A good relat'on between wife and husband –
Hav'ng castles in metropolitan cities –
Great respect in his office and home –
No charges of indiscipline in office –
Or any issue of misappropriation –
Nor charges of disobedience –
He's satisfied with what he has got to date.

Living in a big joint family, not heartily;
Lacking any one issue to be survived;
Above fifty without deficiency;
All possible treatments by famous doctors;
By all, whoever said to contact;
Doing everything possible by them;
Waiting for a child to survived.
All hopes were shatter'd, but a time to cease.

Getting zero chance for conceiving –
Suggested by one to contact a sage.
Becoming ready with some hesitations;
Thinking about its possibility;
Because their previous loss of faith
As doctors have failed to award a child.

Though they meet the sage falling on his feet,
"O Baba, we have all things except a child
In my lap for which we try all around.
Now you are the only hope who can award –
One issue to survive my dynasty –
For dying in peace and rest, and in light."
So, looking at them, from bottom to top
And closing his wet eyes for some minutes,
He said, "There is no issue in your fate.
If you wish, I can award to survive.
But really, after your issue, no issue."
"Aha! Now! *A drowning man catches a straw,*

O sage! Award me in the name of Faith."
"Go, within a year a son in the lap."
All occurs, but his son is issueless
As it has been predicted by the sage.

Spiritual Engineering

For destroying a big temple in Deo –
Of Sun God figured by Lord Vishwakarma;
Where a ruler visited with workers.
The devotee king came and said to him
For not doing so as he could not live
Without Him, and would sacrifice his life.
"In His honour, I urge not to destroy;
I am one of the devotees of Sun God."
The ruler said, "Really, you mundane people,
Worship stones as your determiner."
The king said about the power of the Sun God.
Saying to change the door from east to west,
At night, if Sun God has any power.
All his workers went to pass the night –
Expecting to destroy the next morning,
But the devotee king came to the temple
At night with a sword and sat alone praying
To do wonder and show the world.
The night was to pass on till midnight,
There was no change in the door direction.
Getting it, he said to show His miracle
Within minutes, or he would cut his throat
In the same temple, and before Sun God.
Taking the sword in his hand to do so,
As he set its edge to the throat to cut,
Within a moment there was a loud voice
Coming from a sphere, as it would be collapsed.
But the king continued sitting without fear
And the temple began to move slowly
From right to left, its door turned to the west –
Fully in three hours without any labour –
Through spiritual engineering –
Showing one of God's wonders for full faith.
The Muslim ruler arrived in the morning,
But he went back colourless in God's fear.

Souls to Heaven

A holy place of the Goddess of Power,
Where devotees go in thousands each year
During the first to ninth of Durgapuja –
Where they offer piglets to the goddess
Throwing in the sky in Her name for sake.
But before falling to the ground they all die.
People think about the reason for death
In the sky before coming to the ground,
Where fair science fails and faith survives.
Aha! It is always in the glass of faith.

They Get Who Stand and Wait

Lone, they get who stand righteously and wait;
While all others' requests for only rebate
By God is dismissed soon without mercy;
And all remained drowned in fancy.
God does not deal with anything like people –
Not to give and take, or to face-to-face –
Or to hand to hand as bankers deal –
Though God is always just and handles well –
And everything comes well to those, who wait.

Life is not as we witness before our eyes –
Life is long, and only a few understand –
Innocent childhood, young age of fancy;
Surely on the tattered coat in old age –
All are coined in one, and not separable.
This is the name of real life which we see.
Both joys and sorrows – winter and summer –
And the cold moonlight and the hot sunlight –
Hands towards a friend, again to enemies –
In consideration and formation –
Between man and man, whatever he is –
All life-living activities lifelong –
Different turns in life in course of time –
All is unknown, and in the dark, till they come.

But only ignorant men claim they know.
But they know nothing and live in darkness –
Time changes – as everything except God –
Aha! Man on the boat, and the boat on man –
Time witnesses all this before its eyes –
Surely, once the time comes to all for this turn –
So, a man comes on the boat, and then a man, too –
The man, who is out of the boat, loses all –
The man, who is not righteous, loses all.
Lone, they get those who stand righteously and wait.

Male Empowerment

Once all were for women's empowerment
As of frequent violence against women
By men in each and every walk of life.
But now also for men's empowerment
As such cases are coming to the police
For the violence of women against men.
Yes, this is not a puzzle, but a fact,
And now more than six thousand calls for help
To the police in one year in one state.

According to a survey, the facts came
That violence against women is much more –
Eighty times more than violence against men –
But most are matrimonial complaints –
For which so many comments have been known.
Those cases are frequently lodged in its name
Hiding all the realities of distinction
As it suits better than any other laws
Against men in the Indian penal code –
Frequently revealed exploitation.

A new trend is seen on the court campus,
Of men and women for justice –
As a wife for husband, or husband for wife
Now a wife with a knife ready to erase;
And only the court can save her rage
In the phase of lack of faith in morality –
As the family matter is played as a game
Of football, badminton, chess, and cricket
Forgetting that peace and pleasure reside
In their heart and understanding,
Not in the court of law or in the field,
Where wrong desires of men and women shine
Taking legal evils instead of virtues.
Sex, love, and marriage are now played as games
For pleasure forgetting, keeping aside all;
Considering virtue and evil are the same.
One feels pleasure doing so, not shame;

Moving in courts as centenary trains;
Forgetting men and women are two sides
Of the same coin for continuation
Of the creation with their beauty;
And without anyone, the world is barren –
For the fair world, fair society to us –
And for its fairness, fair procreation;
And for fair procreation fair practices
Of love, sex and marriage are too needful.
Ignoring all this now they move into courts
For love and pleasure – for peace and justice
Just like a refugee who does in camps;
As a thirsty man, on the sand for water;
As a jeweller in a forest for pearls;
As a saint in town for meditation –
Leaving his lonely shed in the forest.

The Widow in Tears

With salt-blood flowing, she presses on,
Her lover's death left her so woebegone,
In youthful days when joy was near at hand.
Her sailor gone, her life unmanned –
Left to endure endless sorrow and woe.
Nights greet her like the devil's show –
Days call her to the court of trial –
She faces suffering's unending dial
With no explanation on her side,
Alone she stands to face the tide –
A trial, no lawyers to defend,
No facts or acts to comprehend.

All this because of the loss,
Of the one with whom she shared love's gloss.
Now he's gone, leaving her to despair,
Her heart scorched, she bears the flare.

Nights come like shocks of current's might –
In her youth – once full of delight,
Now absorbing pains and constant chains.
Misfortunes stalk her like night-time owls;
Others prowl like tigers on their prowls.
Men seek her for their lustful wants,
Expecting her surrender, seeking fun
Yet she gets cooperation from none.
Recalls her joyful days with him –
Now she burns and boils, a true victim.
Her life's a struggle, strife all around;
Tears and tears, in sorrow she's bound.

A Father in Triangles

A father is not free but in triangles –
The triangles of food, clothes, and house –
The triangles of three educated sons –
Criminal, adulterer, and gambler –
All evil under the sun is fun.
He is a teacher and a gentleman,
With fair character and sound knowledge
Which is not significant at this age.

He is ill but has no one to serve him now;
Though he did all for his sons as he could
Providing education and good culture.
But only for food, he moves door to door –
He expects from this house to that house –
None to change his clothes on rainy days
And three houses he made, not in his reach.
A shed is enough for him as his sons think.
No one to administer medicine,
Or to offer food, except to torture,
Or defame any way doing wrong deeds.
They are also in service, but no fame
Except to embrace evil wherever.
Leaving no option they live roughly
And their father in unique triangles.

Gandhi the Deliverer

Love and Truth never die – God never dies;
He is ever alive – all can see Him.
He is present here at each bidding speed!
All to eliminate Him are vividly dead –
Assassins, their ideology and community,
Everyone is behind their conspiracy.
And they all will never rise or grow.
All failed to kill Him with their bullets –
He is ever alive, but they are dead,
Who doesn't know "they themselves have been killed"
As their thousands of years of sin or monopoly –
All this has been burnt by Him completely.
There are several devoted followers
Who will further His mission and vision –
Who'll continue to work for righteousness?

He arrived to abolish all sins –
To end the Darkness of Ignorance –
To replace with Truth and Ahimsa everywhere –
Among the heart and mind of all mankind –
To abolish all evils of the world –
And to restore virtues to the broad world –
To restore full faith in the Maker –
To award such a power as for saints –
To settle righteousness everywhere –
To prevail over Light and to end the Darkness –
To seal the Ignorance of all mankind
To teach the value of morality and truth,
To restore love, peace, prosperity,
Justice, compassion, and religious duty
As is done by a magician at a time –
As is like the effect of the Divine –
Like the bliss that is in the heavenly state.
Aha! Peace and peace and bliss too, all around!

Man and Nature

I came alone to you and joined soon –
You are indeed as cool and calm as the moon.
You are on a flower, I on duty –
Only for my huge pocket's beauty.

You are little, but a symbol of joy;
You have neither partiality nor coy;
You're my only impartial friend
While all others care for joy in the trend.

I used to get a chair from my due ward
And sit near the red flower of your bard,
And enjoy the charms of natural life
Forgetting the beauty of strife.

You usually go somewhere for some time,
I go to the class to fulfil the prime.
You deliver completely natural joys;
But I spread my vain knowledge to boys.

My knowledge fountain is fully mortal;
Your blissful song is fairly immortal;
I teach all from dark and painful pages;
But you deliver divine joys for ages.

Mine is worldly – in a mortal order
But your holy chant not to thunder,
When you chant, I forget all miseries
And when I deliver, everyone wearies.

O Prophet, very soon release man from woes!
Because now all shade them from knowledge vows!
You read and pour the holy pages of Nature;
I get and deliver vain things of pleasure.

O nightingale, you forgot after years.
So I find nothing, but only hot tears.
Neither you nor any of the kin is here
And without your aid, now I only fear.

You now forget the flower of my state;
And I enjoy the deadly charms of my fate.
No expectation for change in the sphere.
O immortal bird! Now can I live here?

The Invitation Fee

True to the fact that everything changes;
The climate changes – man also changes;
Forgetting each thing – either right or wrong;
Remembering material gain and bliss;
Desiring never to miss or dismiss.
Now everything is a thing of the game –
The way of honour and hospitality –
In the past, the guest was indeed a god;
But now as a traveller to pay due;
Who buys tickets on counters for a journey;
Paying sum to dry and hard officials.
The same is now to pay respect to guests
And flourishing all around in fashion;
Several counters and officials too;
With notebooks as students keep in classrooms
Where their names and sums are clearly mentioned
As mentioned by cashiers in banks.

On the occasions of marriage or else
The counters are decorated to collect.
Paying its fees they move further for food
As the passengers go to bogies
After purchasing the proper tickets;
Coupons are issued to them in their fame.
One is invited to earn maximum money
Along with getting gifts for the kith;
Inviting all persons – known or unknown.
Unable to decline as he is boss
They are his salaried subordinates
Where there's no chance to decline his fine
As all others are under his regime.
Peons or officers – all in the race;
None is a way to get the grace to win,
Otherwise the cold relation in the future.

The Midnight Saint

He was a criminal before midnight
And who has just stolen a golden bell
From a nearby temple of the white fame
Breaking the iron door in thick darkness.
The charges of theft, robbery, and murder;
Several times in jail marches he held
Several times he's beaten by the police,
He was in search of a religious trademark
To conceal his old fame, so none could blame him –
To grow like some godmen in the country.
Willing to change and discover ways;
Coming to light that the maroon garments
And long beards can settle as a great sage;
The best way to age for high earning
Without any kind of tax and records.
Neither the goods and service tax nor loss.
He gets up with a vision in the morn –
Wearing maroon garments and with a view
Not to come back to his home forever
And to live in the shed that he has made;
As a sage with the miracles to bless all
Who comes to him for a nominal fee?

"God has awarded me boon at midnight –
Now you will do undone and done undone."
He begins the new service as a saint
And challenges to curing any disease
Under the sun and the moon of all here
Without any medicine, rather by boon
Which God has awarded only to him.
He starts religious trade, leaving his old works
And doing the same in new ways to hide;
Living in the monastery of million;
Fairies all around him as in heaven;
Challenging to turn sorrows into joy
Whoever lives with him alone at night
For seven days in his personal room.

The Lover's Review

He felt love is never a cheap passion
As an easy and general practice
To use and throw whenever one desires.
He used and threw as he could in life
But while reviewing he feels it was lust
In the name of love only to defame.
Love, as all do, is not love but rather lust
Because of sexual excitement
That is mortal with an animal passion;
It's not the love like Savitri and Satyavan;
Or love like Alcestis and Admetus.
It's trimming the root and nearing the lust;
Forgetting the values and morality
For sexual pleasure for the time being.
He escaped in a one-night passion of lust
Losing his peace and rest and relatives;
Placing at the hands of cruel repentance;
Leaving all things which were to be done;
One terrible decision to elope
And to settle anywhere as per will.

He only pines for the past and no chance.
He now reviews his past and his future
Suggesting all the young generation
To strengthen the faith in love not in lust
And never to practice lust in its name
To defame and blur in any manner.
He has escaped breaking all ties;
Ignoring the pious institution
Of marriage practiced ov'r the world
In different ways but for the same view.
He wrote a letter to their parents
To excuse and let them join the family –
The young generation doesn't repeat
As they had practiced and lost everything.

The Walk for Justice

Economically poor – rich in spirit;
Rather a man of strong will and divine light;
Ever agree to fight against evil;
Never looking back for taking rest;
Occupying only a few metres of land
That was his means of livelihood;
Connected to a small mud-built cottage;
Living with the members of his family
And his wife serves in others' kitchen
With her four minor children to foster.
He followed social and moral values
And without any blame for his fame.

A superman captured his total land.
No one came to help against injustice.
He tried hard for justice but loses everywhere
All the courts and officers against him
Who purchased law, courts, and officers.
A miracle occurred with a fresh trial.
The special court revises all cases
Of the victim and holding them guilty.
Finally, he wins and all others lose –
Truth won and all evil is washed away.

Between Man and God

Once he was a thief and was known for theft;
Then he chose to operate cyber crimes,
Is arrested many times for this.
Coming from jail and getting a place
In a famous temple in the country
To an unknown place with a new level
Presenting as a man of the priestly caste;
He is appointed a temple priest.
Presenting himself an agent for God –
A man between man and God to God-lead –
He began to steal sums from donations –
Also stole golden statues of deities
Enjoyed many fairies in his cell.
He prepared to be the head of the trust –
All acts were known so he went back home
Where he got a temple of great fame
Declaring himself as celibate –
Winning the confidence of devotees
And getting success in his new business –
Occupying the business of sacrifice
Moving several places in a year
For the collection of many donations.
He hoarded money in lacs every year
Without any fear, tax, and ransom sum.
He's a saint but works as a robber.

Wearing maroon clothes from top to bottom
He seems like a saint and a path-finder.
He begins the trade of temple building
In each village with a new view to earn
More than anyone in a company.
He becomes a priest in a big temple
And setting a number of loudspeakers –
He plays twenty hours out of twenty-four.
While all others complain about his move;
Saying not to play any louder
As it heavily creates sound pollution.

But he mutters alone in his defence,
"If there's no pollution in the area
No disease will cause them, and all will be glad.
If no one is sick, who will come for a boon
To temples for the deities' blessing.
If they don't come, my profession will die.
If it dies, I'll die, so I do for me.
I sit under the cabin, and no voice comes.
If students read in peace, they'll get good marks
For obtaining good jobs in other parts
And they will go out, leaving this sour place.
If they leave, who will come here for blessings?
A matter of trade I will never lose;
Whatever they tell me or criticize.
I'll continue to execute my trade –
Either anyone is happy or unhappy.
All have rights to do any right or wrong."

A Tramp Woman

She used to go read as a student;
But getting the golden chance she desires
To enhance her relationship with a boy
Of her own study centre and circle.
"Look at me, a fruit full of juice and flesh;
Tastier than any other fruits in the world."
He sees, hugs and kisses, thrice embraces
And taking her to his lap step by step,
He did what they needed to do at the time.
Turning it into a daily routine;
Considering it a boon, not a crime.
She married to one another young man,
Though not to live for formality.
Going there, she began to play the game
Of immorality and family strife –
Blaming her in-laws – declining to live.
Returning she lodged many cases
In the local court against her in-laws
With the complete support of her parents;
Thinking that he would skyrocket their fame
That is written only in her name.

Getting him killed brutally, she lived right
With her parents, enjoying her lovers.
She acted widely in the wide fair of lust;
But for her, it is fair if true love.
She married twice, a man over sixty
And fell in lust with her married stepson.
It is known by her step daughter-in-law
And she is rooted by them finally.
Then she begins to love a neighbour boy;
But the same was known, so she eloped;
Escaping to an unknown place to live
She embraced several men in life;
They enjoyed her body charm or she enjoyed it.
But at last, she comes to punish her show.

She's arrested but expects all is well –
Remembering her last lover for a boon.
"Mr Paul, now I am on the way to jail
And you can only release me from hell."
"O, I expect you will be close to me
When I close my wet eyes for the next world."

The Nine-Coloured Saint

In a true sense, he was a clothed global man,
And choosing the dress he thought very deeply –
"What should be the best dress for me?" –
"Should I have the special clothes and place too?"
For his industry, he spoke joyfully –
"White for leaders, green for one, red for saints,
Black for a magician – and for me?"
"I am a saint! Red for religious motives,
Blue for a political party, mixed for a mob,
Maroon for traditional saints. What for me?
Which colour suits me? The best for me!"
"O my God, right I'm! Indeed soon I found.
It represents everyone – I know everything
And I'll preach lessons to everyone easily."

He got a nine-coloured long dress stitched.
There was no problem with the presentation.
People said, "He was a 'Nine-coloured saint'!"
They asked him, "From where you have come?"
"I frequently used to deliver lessons
On the top of the Himalayas near the Sage."
So they regarded him a great saint.
They were quite unaware of his black acts –
Robbery, blackmailing, rape, murder, fraud, theft –
Quite unmentionable, but so many facts.

He became the chief of the monastery –
The chief of the hundred acres of land –
Gold in quintals with the large apartment,
He began to repeat his deeds of the past,
And he got his junior seer killed too,
He enjoyed many women, who were full fair,
And he gave them gold and diamond too much,
And devotees did not know of his black acts.
But the police knew his all secret works,
And arrested from a luxurious hotel
With his double beloveds watching blue films.
He said, "Political leaders want to blame

Because I am in the top seat of fame.
All of the countries are aware of me –
Of the holy acts of Nine-coloured saint."

Pleasure in Evil

The principal said to submit the list,
So he could continue to feel the taste.
But getting the list of many useful books
He was fired to see his red looks.

Convincing too, to do the same to gain;
Otherwise, the pocket remains in vain.
He suggests recommending such a book
That will decorate the shelf with its look.

He always said to buy from old stores
That will fully fulfil all golden hopes.
If not following his path to growing fast
He tells all that now the service is last.

For a number of problems, he awards all,
Compelling absolutely to fall;
Others are black and he, a Brahmin white.
So has he gained such a worldly right?

His intention is to harass;
So he participates in evil class.
Following the tradition of the age,
But never approved by the sage.

Cannibalism

Man is the meanest being, none believes,
But inhumane acts in Noida reveal
Showing man's thirst and hunger for man's blood;
The skeletons of poor men are in the mud.

It doesn't show everything about man's act
Rather one of the inner aspects of fact.
A man in a luxurious bungalow
Who kills and sells their organs – not a flaw?

It is not all or the end of a goblin;
In this big organ trade, so many set in.
More than five hundred boys become one's prey
But none knows his large slaughter for money.

The police said mercilessly to one,
"You breed many kids, so let them go in vain."
Are the police or government responsible?
By powerful men, is it bearable?

Does one get its answer? Only they know –
Whose children become prey of the man's vow.
For months and years, their parents are in search
But unable, and they find in the drains' ditch.

It reflects man's inner heart and thirst;
It absolutely claims man's greed and lust.
Only Noida doesn't reflect what is man.
But better Noida proves which he began.

All such deeds confirm that life has no fee,
Everything is joyless, whatever men see.
Tiger in the form of Man, in this age,
And one tries best only to erase.

Dear Death

Dear Death! You kill only who are to depart –
Not, who has even some time to take part.
You ruin the hopes which are illusive –
Never, whoever is sure and successive.

You dispose of the desires of man's core
Who thinks about only more and more –
You ever limit endless and vain joys –
And forbid hardships and limitless noise.

As you welcome one, no need for houses;
Or of food or milk, of red and black cows;
Or the box of multi-colour rupees;
Or any award or honour trophies.

You end any type of use of a rod
Or the heavily locked treasure of a fund;
All forget low and high types of sound
Dear Death! The suffering does not hound.

Without any kind of fare, you send all there,
Where is a divine House, that seems too bare?
Nothing veiled; all free and no colour;
No caste or race; the seen House forever.

The Curse of Cow

You move in each street as a hawker
And carry milk in your body like a bucket.
Men behave cruelly as a big shocker;
They turn and treat you as a milk locket.

Previously, they milked you at their home,
And now you are milked to a customer.
Now your ease, and life; all is gloom,
And red milk is taken out by the producer.

Once you known as a mother, a goddess;
Now not more than a machine as your face –
You are dealt with the people as spiritless
Giving delicious food that all can mess.

Not A Man of Mercy?

How much a considerable work on earth?
Who is hanged for global man's mirth?
A huge crowd assembles to see the show
As all this is done to fulfil one's vow.

Death-time is too painful for all beings;
In the morning, they're present there, in rings;
But no mercy, they told him, "God damn you.
We are here to enjoy it, which was due."

When he's set on the scaffold for hanging
They're enjoying, chanting, and singing.
No word to reflect such a sinful work;
They forget, "They're also for the same dark."

He's happy to pass the gateway of life;
The men of the opposite sect were with a knife;
The security of home and foreign rule;
Anyway, they reached there as the cell was full.

The then government got a film made of his footage
To keep a record of its carnage.
At the moment of death, all of our shock –
But people were present only to mock.

Saddam boldly said, "I offer my soul to God.
You've to live under a miserable sod."
Their mockery of his sentence was no mean.
Has each one not gone to a set place?

Bribery

Going there for issuing a passport;
The documents are in a lot;
Columns are clearly made, no chance to bet
But the clerk holds it in the bribery net.

Filling the application once again,
There's no point in illegal gain.
Getting it he said, "All this is vain.
Get out soon, you must come here at noon."

So visiting there again, he said,
"I have no time to see even your head."
Requesting him to see for the work
But no mercy; he begins to bark.

One visited a round agent for help;
Who moved with him to fulfil his hope,
"Now our time is over, so none can do.
Go for the next day, as no time to boo."

Requesting again, "O my dear cash,
You must see his face, as money is no less;
Now double amounts he is ready to face;
Look at him and see his costly necklace."

He gently takes rupees two-ten hundred
Then gazes and moves his big head;
A new look was of his huge pocket's shade.
Indeed his new-white face was money made.

Injustice

For investigation, a government agency,
But with two eyes – to bite – and for mercy;
One for the rich and another for the poor;
The way of a probe to save who is dear.

One for all the influential men;
Another for all helpless children;
Seventy-nine in a village, a hundred
To five hundred, but you've no tears to shed.

The issue of someone only for fame;
When the media ask you, reply without shame.
O Supreme Agency of the big country!
For the poor a toy – for the rich a sentry.

All people say, "Are you for the poor class?"
You can see your face in the Noida glass;
The same is in other scams of the past;
They also easily scan your drama at last.

They say, "For the rich, you are a puppet;
For the poor, stronger like a hard socket.
Are you a bulky doll to pay them due?
For the sake of the rich, so they thank you?

Tsunami

You are not our enemy, but our friend!
An agent to wash earthly woes and a trend;
Sorrows of many who are known in the name
Of sectarianism and barbarism.

They take a divine bath. Do they repent?
You return very soon. Were you indecent?
No woes, no one opposes, surrenders soon;
An infant in Sri Lanka seemed like the moon –
And who untouched by you, lives to breathe.

In your holy lap, who gets the divine bath;
Forgets forever all woes, anyone hath
The sense of difference; low-high, poor-rich;
Virtuous sinner or anything else to preach?
None to say – none to interrogate – why?

All accept your impartial clutch soon
As your notification is a boon.
All expressed "All's right, no need to fight."
All are unable to oppose your right.
They admit your holy order, saying "thank you."

No woe and secured a divine remedy;
Who's here, he says, "a momentary comedy."
Some are unaware of the comedy by you.
You must come each year to collect all due.
O Tsunami! You're a divine friend indeed.

Time

You are supreme, and you rule over all.
Yes, your art is supreme, others to fall!
Yes, your seat is supreme to monitor!
Yes, your look is supreme to linger!

You are immortal and none is equal
You probe everyone, placing them as mortal;
Nothing in the world without your right date,
All physical become pets and have to obey fate.

You have seen the age of Ram and Ravan,
Also, earth to heaven link that is unseen.
You have seen Judas, Christ, and a Christian;
Your longest sight observes well, not in fun.

Buddha and Mahavira also reached your sight –
The immortal Moses' seat for making neat;
You film all the pioneers forever;
While they all come to you to meet, never.

All pass before your huge immortal eyes;
Gandhi and others died, but none fairly tries.
You know all – truth never dies, or it cries;
But records it well, and all under its ties.

Hitler, Confucius, and several others died;
But you are the same, which all mortal beings find.
Prophets advocate "love", and truth and they pass;
The world is the same, and no shame to harass.

Rose and Love

O rose! O, love! You are of equal race!
You are a rose! You are love! No difference!
An intimate tie between love and rose;
Impossible to live alone as you pose.

None is, who doesn't love a rose-like flower;
O rose! You welcome all with a shower.
Here is your only ray of hope – a ray of love
When one witnesses, his feet don't move.

You are only representative of joy;
A divine balm for bliss, unlike a toy.
Your touch is a divine touch, all e'er say,
And none, in the world, can send you to clay.

Marriage

You're a unique magician and musician;
You're just like a give-and-take technician;
You make alien to own – own to the alien;
Arranging a quite new couple to go on.

You award tears to an alien, love to own –
The fake thing to own and true to alien –
Teasers to own and a friend to teasers –
Woe and anguish to own, to alien, cheers.

House to halt; halt to house, easily able –
Stable to unstable, and revert to all –
A member to alien, to own nothing –
Known to the unknown, and reverting everything.

Embrace to slap, slap to embrace to set.
Indeed, you seem too merciless without a net.
No one blames your art to get too tied
The blot of lesbian and gay are dried.

Holy Embellishments

O holy vermilion! If you are, I am;
You answer each one, showing a new fame.
Beauty is never for the nose but for the look;
Head to nose for a good harmony, no hook.

You do – you make "she and me", "he and I".
You in ears attached to nose to seem shy;
Carbon in both eyes – an overlook of the sight
On lips then seems something more for new might.

Seeing it, minds or reminds, sees-foresees;
Promises divine you remind and close;
And in fingers, a social firmament;
Around the neck a shining ornament.

You in a nail – red and pink for twenty's face
In arms, colour of henna, for the palm dress.
A large diamond look'd for the feet finger;
Anklets around the ankle for a clinger.

Mosquito

Now, not an insect that sucks blood only;
A fate creator books a ticket calmly;
Once notorious only for malaria;
Now you can dispatch a man from the area.

Once only a night singer and dancer;
Now in daylight, also a woe launcher.
A net was enough for the dark night's sleep
But now coils and liquid go into deep.

At night, you sing a long musical song;
And attempting magically lifelong;
Per year take lives of the thousands of men;
And children, surrender before you like a hen.

Government policy for its sake on paper;
Move around, and suck blood from the deep layer.
O mosquito! O encephalitis! God of death!
People fear and they have no faith.

Only for Money

Reaching there in time for work with a friend;
Fully unaware of the office trend
While a request for a certificate.
He smiled and said, "On time, you will bet".

Fairly submitting the application
Because never got an "Indian lesson".
The clerk said smiling, "If you have to get,
The bribe mercy you will have to set."

"Listen, rupees a thousand if before noon,
And half if you need it afternoon,
Or know, it's two-thirds till the midnight's bell,
Happily, it is quarter for the next day's call."

But rupees were paid to him, five hundred
For securing his hot blessings' bear shed;
The money-making story of the bar council;
Wonderfully, the task was all uphill.

Spoon Games

Now all games are played in a room easily
By which we glorify winner fame fairly –
Battle, boating, football, skating, cricket,
Badminton, card, and chess, all in a set.

There is no role of the body, but rather of the mind;
Uses of eyes and fingers, but not of hand;
Only one finger, not two, but all clean;
Fixing serious eyes only on the screen.

Not going anywhere to play for wealth;
Or to face the scorching sun or on a heath;
One alone plays happily to win a shield;
And there is no need to play in a field.

Completely free from physical exercise,
But treads the world high score, seems he is wise.
What is a video game? For a sound body?
All say for making the body too cloudy.

Such skills are absolutely best friends
Of such companies, which grow fast with trends;
Only increasing the doctors' big pockets,
But no one says, "They play with the dark nets'"

Depression or diabetes is also seen;
Some many do not digest and only groan,
Taking different medicines, more to rack –
Or to fulfil the need of a sick stomach.

Enhancing the income of any company;
Although the pocket is down in lack of money.
Previously, going to the field for exercise,
But now those who play video games, are too wise.

In the past, played dramas, and also their roles;
But now they are the parts of disease holes –
They acted, danced and participat'd in race;
Now, all this is a thing of video grace.

Riding, sheep fighting, and bull game were for fame;
Presently, they are great matters of shame.
Video games are indeed only for names;
And all round reluctance for all old games.

The Discount System

A culture or a system, but not in a shop
As an old fashioned beaten-broken lyre,
Rather prevalent for a joyful future hope
In government offices they all hire.

The system is prevalent in each office –
Among employees on low and high posts
The situation is critical, but no sacrifice
For solution and they do without dots.

The sum of tax is released as a grant;
But it is fully drunk by officials;
But for them, there is no call or warrant;
For bribes, they look ever at clock dials.

Money is released for the works of welfare;
But it begins to descend like a beam;
And all participate in this holy fair;
Officials shine – the public work is dim.

Getting commission, up to ninety per cent;
Ten per cent for the purpose, but no shame;
The system, prevalent in courageous bent;
And for each work, one has to donate.

Making most officials too rich
While the public turn lean and thin.
The systems of the government they munch;
In competition, honesty goes in vain.

Enhancing the sale of red English wine;
It is a fashion as the law is vain;
And for remedy of fatty, they pay fine;
But no turn as all try for maximum gain.

The Disco Walk

The ways of morning walks, now of a folk,
On a metalled road with rosy hooked shoes;
Trousers deep and colourful, polished talk,
Along with flowery marks on tattoos.

Not only on the chest but also on his back;
Not a folk cut, but rather touching to heart,
The cap mosaic on his head while on a walk –
And his language is rhetorical to flirt!

Not on foot, but by a bike or a car;
Hours pass in the cheap side hotel to furnish.
This is the modern way for his health war.
Not for his body, but only to tarnish.

Live and Let Live

A prevalent culture in offices
To upgrade bribery, but no grievances.
It is a known system of percentage –
Either low to high – all in this age as sage.

Top to bottom, and without shame, all do.
If undone, the files are thrown into the loo,
And the law is oft followed partially;
They continue to upgrade it heartily.

If not in the trend, means being a mean man;
In the trade, he's oft regarded unfit;
He in his service without promotion
And his life without bribery lotion.

He is unable to wash his garment's moss,
And as always to remain at a great loss;
Some say proudly, "It is Indians' main part,
So all servants participate in this art."

The Mobile Zone

In past years, the mobile zone, city to city;
Now outdoor to the kitchen – man to a deity.
In the same house, dining room to the bedroom –
Bathroom to a yard, and also to out-shed.

In the future, definitely bed to bed,
It is not fiction, but a true mind's made.
The zone is of an insurance manager;
Not only one but many play with danger.

Coming to the outdoors, he waits and dials;
The door is opened, and proudly he enters.
From the bathroom, he informs his gender
Bring a napkin, or, also underwear.

Coming out, he dials and demands a hot meal,
It's his lifestyle and the homely deal.
As he comes back, dials his office;
Going to the office plays mobile voice.

The same event repeats when he takes a rest;
Also while he's driving to his best.
Proudly, he says, "I have never had to pay,
The office pays, so I do anyway".

A True Leader

A true leader is now, who anyhow leads;
The second feature is who best delivers;
For the fulfilment of his aim, who beats,
And to tell a lie, he never forgets.
Who does not cheat is indeed no leader;
If necessary, he moves to murder.
Who is prosperous, and who uses wide snares,
And he knows defalcating techniques.
The best is who, as he can, gets bribes,
And if getting any chance, who also rapes,
And a true leader is, one who wreaks havoc –
The greatest is who is unrealistic.

Official Bills

The computer-printed bills on paper;
And supplied by a well-known supplier;
Of the best quality in the local market,
But really the lowest of a kind to bet.

The large amount paid at the highest rate
From the shops that pay the commission best.
Stickers smile and say, "The work is very good."
But things are like waste items, indeed.

Sometimes shops are unaware of the supply,
Before auditors, they smile like dye;
Taking the dose of bribe, they say, all's well.
Otherwise, objecting, they go to hell.

Money suggests them for such types of bills;
Excites much to participate in such drills.
If bills are true, they flatly say, "rubbish";
Disagreeing, they say for bills "girlish."

Official Sympathy

This is no human sympathy, office sage.
But it is in the office at this age!
Know, it's not classical, but rather modern!
After the appointment, all employees learn.

"If one does, others do as devotees.
If you do not give, I'll not foresee.
Give and take, throw and get, and sow and reap.
If not given, the work is short or deep.
Files not in hand, the scarcity of time,
Shortage of paper, shortcomings – no prime;
The red Gandhi currency completes files,
And suggests them to go soon, even miles.
It's a symbol of freedom, as Gandhi is
The father of the nation; so follow, please.
Enjoying freedom for a facility fee.
And destroying all legal norms for glee
Is this a bribe or a gratuity?
The practice of clerks without honesty.
Not only for them, teachers and doctors also
Saying it is wrong, but we do to glow.
Are they merciful? Taking what they do for you.
Throw and get, give and take, for anyone's view.
Or sleep and suffer. Do you? Know, all this!
Or no one will ask, and you'll have to miss."

The Smokeless Industry

India is progressive, each one believes;
New education system fully drinks
As leaded petrol in a big factory;
And a few understand its mystery.

All this is like large-scale industry;
Now education in a factory;
The centre has to provide knowledge –
Awards degrees, but no light of the age.

Now developing management's health;
Now only enlarging students' strength –
Bothers in the name of education;
All wonders seeing its situation.

Previously all for education;
But now only for fashion –
Glooming fast the holy brow of wisdom –
And money-making machine of one's kingdom.

Not a study place, but a factory –
In one's interest, one runs an industry.
The admission is on paper in blue ink,
Where students' wisdom is only to shrink.

The centre enlarges the accounts' shape,
There is no sign of knowledge on a scholar's map.
Only to make management richer
In the name of providing education cheaper.

It ruins easily all education rules;
Wasting the education of basic clues;
All as large wine shops and evening jokes;
Seeing even a rickshaw puller mocks.

A fruit of liberalization –
Turning education into a fashion –
From where cent per cent of students get degrees,
Without toil, only for ceremonies.

Institutes in thousands pollute brains,
And in a record, the students in millions.
Attempting hard to pollute our nation
Decorating those who study fashion?

The Fortunate Leader

Many riots between two communities
Because of an issue around deities;
When great violence and bloodshed all around;
Where a lot were victims of communal cloud.

Before the riots, he was a rickshaw puller –
Later became a democracy driller.
Where many communities praised him
As Hercules and Achilles were too dim.

Becoming the master of his religion,
He was arrested and sent to prison.
After a month he came out of jail
Because the Supreme Court granted his bail.

Getting the ticket to a high party;
He was elected to make the house dirty.
After a week, he made money for a car;
Later a house like Ajanta for a bar.

In one year, a democracy puller;
All items in his house became clearer,
His supporters' zeal in a cooler;
The law and order making over clear.

A number of riots break out in a year;
Hundreds of people easily become God's dear;
Elected three times for the assembly
He continues to drink politics fully.

Elected twice for parliament;
People support his riot sacrament;
His language and garments like fine silk,
He always uses and drinks political milk.

During the riots, he threw dead in drains,
Who were revealed and removed by cranes.
No doubt, he knows the rate of democracy
Doing all to fulfil his fancy.

Many innocent persons are sent to jail –
Outwardly, he enjoys political smell.
There's no loss for him, even in any nail;
But many innocent people go to hell.

Modern Honesty

Selling virtues and gaining for pocket –
Classical honesty don't set with it.
One comes to the Sports Superintendent
As the net was torn and wanted to get.

He gives and says, "except this nothing" –
It's in the stock and no other setting.
"Do you not know? Sir, I pay fees each year.
Nothing in the stock – all become your dear."

Rather the net of badminton is old,
Which was torn, broken, and also rolled.
Really, nine times, sports items were purchased;
On the paper, the big stock was dressed.

Recording the stock of rupees nine lac –
But on his face, there is no ray of shock.
During the long term, his wealth enhanced
Continuing to gain his pocket's demand.

The whole term awarded him two vehicles –
Ruining all virtues as law killers –
Looking as an ambassador of state –
And the several things he enjoys to date.

His house is full of the latest items;
But payers become the pet of systems.
The making of problems in his interests –
Doing all right or wrong for pockets.

A Student

With modern-cuts hair and all in the fair;
Half long or short, with a short shirt and pants
Like the blouse of a trench on honeymoon –
Hardly falls to waist to cover the skin.

Colourful pants with a polished sticker –
Many pockets like a bunch of a flower –
Two behind the knee and without any last –
Two on the buttocks only to go fast.

A flower, one to every – on the sleeve;
On both the lower parts of the pants to sieve;
A hooked cap on the head as Boy Darcy,
And film stars smile, only to get mercy.

The polished hooked shoes with the high heel,
The mixed colour which anyone can feel;
Fanciful socks like an ambassador
Without good conduct and character.

The perfume of rose creates wonder
With a costly smart phone and a long wire
To connect hot blue film while reading,
Tackling the book as he is driving.

The notebook with image of a fair star –
Not of a simple star, but from a bar –
With the disco smile, a pen of gel ink
Where all virtue can easily sink.

Absolutely, "he for she"; "she" for "he"
With a strong desire to suck as a bee;
Now all the students only in this state
Waiting to secure the outcome of fate.

The Civic Sense

Pollution is a great problem of the age,
But all take it easy in their craze.
Scientists suggest us oft decrease,
But some continue their attempts to increase.

Governments and public try to control,
But some pollute the atmosphere and fall;
Frequent slogans to maintain cleanliness,
Due to ignorance, all this is meaningless.

Several throw dust into the dustbin;
The landlord says to throw it into the drain
Issuing an order to fill fully the hole
Where there's no civic sense or any control.

The Buffet System

A modern system in our modern culture
For eating and standing like a vulture
Like long rough rows at the railway station –
While feet start to ache due to the fashion.

Some are pushed forward fast to get –
Some to overtake for the belly fate.
Who get are regarded as luckier than those
Who do not get it because of a new pose?

Those who qualify in a pre-test, start to eat –
When lacking, they try to fulfil their seat –
They begin to roam all around to drink –
When there's no chance, their hope begins to sink.

Some get over the dish and fail to eat,
But no shame they feel, rather too fit.
Who gets half a dish, the stomach suffers
But who gets an over dish, the body aches.

Now a regarded culture for all men,
Those who do not follow it have to fall;
Who doesn't accept it is considered a fool –
Folk, rustic, uncultured, backward, and cool.

There's each and every item to complete
In the competition for a dish hit,
Many have a warm attitude to embracing it
But some have a blind attitude to hate it.

Dreams

Some fail to provide things for relation;
No one has command over creation,
The atmosphere of pollut'on is on earth,
As all mankind attempts to do for mirth.

The pollution of water, air, and sound
Are caused by industries to ground;
The care that all this is taken by no one;
The civic sense is a matter of fun.

The heat is increasing because of smoke;
The frozen part of the world is ready to mock;
The green part is, too, for fulfilling food;
And now Nature is used to change our mood.

Men worship the rivers as goddesses;
Many fields lack water, and someone dies;
The cuss of fire in rainy times is seen,
All are unaware. Who is mean?

All programmes are on stages, not on grounds;
Long lectures are delivered among crowds;
Innocent men suffer, and die without grant;
Many troubles ended with a death warrant.

Who's responsible for it, live in rest;
Those irresponsible, suffer best.
The pollution is worse than pesticides,
Which has made us ill, and none unifies.

It's not a dream, but rather a war in the age
"To throw the pages of science and knowledge –
Just to go back to Nature to erase –
To abolish the tragedy of this phase."

"God must send angels to waste factories;
We must go forward to save all countries.
O God! Promise to change, not day by day;
Rather, next morning, all will play."

Registration for Mars

There is darkness and darkness everywhere;
None is safe – none is free here and all dare
To kill at any moment, but no wonder;
If a woman is raped, no wonder;
The property is robb'd in broad daylight;
All are agreeable and none wishes to fight.
Alone telling one, We live in India;
A place, where corruption is an idea –
Here, freedom is accurate without rate;
Where criminals boldly enjoy their fate;
Where every walk of life is full of pain;
The best place to use might be mighty men.

Freedom for anything and no restriction –
To murder and rape to fulfil fashion.
A man is rich or influential here;
But on Mars all is right, where a few there;
Where able men preparing to manage
To enjoy the blessings of the new sage.

God is Deaf

God is supreme, who looks into all here;
For Him, nothing is dark, each thing is bare.
But many think to convince Him better
Their works on Earth use loudspeakers.

For securing a special award –
Giving high sounds in mosques, temples, and a bard.
Its price is not more but reasonable;
Million times more, for those, who're unable.

Its sound awards pollution everywhere,
Someone thinks "God is a student to hear."
Now raising several wars against Nature,
Wasting all resources, a great wonder.

Modernism

Money is heaven, a fair body for a man;
Money and a body in the hands of a woman,
Willing to break the knot before marriage;
Man accepts woman for his sex garage.

Man loves the skin of animals, never animals;
And placing him greater than cannibals.
But none loves a man if a man lives virtuously;
After death, man is loved by man heartily.

Before death, man hates man as he's a beast
Man's portrait is loved, considering him chaste.
A husband hasn't one, but many more options;
A wife isn't a whore, who does in fashions.

The look of the body is well-painted by all;
Ignoring the will of the soul as a doll;
Ceasing man's soul in his body as a slave
While it has a strong will to rule and crave.

Everything is money as a new vision;
Virtue is no matter for decision.
Now, man is the greatest enemy of man;
And money is the best friend of everyone.

The worst is honoured, the best is abused;
Evil is liked and virtue is stupid.
Now placing film stars as gods in this age;
Deities are worshipped on the big stage.

But Not a Prophet

You seem greater with ivory,
And none can feel your deeds in a hurry.
Your words are creamy but seem a devil
Partaking in black acts and each evil.

"I am born in the city of Harishchandra,
And Lord Shiva not to loot or to withdraw;
Holding such a post not to rob or to shoot,
But for the works of welfare, not to loot."

Looking as a prophet, you are not clean
As the employees of college have seen.
You are white in the face, running in the race
Using the college for years under pace.

Only doing one work – twenty-four hours;
Remaining busy with sum showers.
Retired, the college became a corpse,
But no shame to you when you see its moss.

You went but left your followers to use;
Now only one of nonsense, who has no dues.
May God pardon you for all the black acts.
Although, always ignored the well-known facts!

www.ingramcontent.com/pod-product-compliance
Lightning Source LLC
Chambersburg PA
CBHW030133260626

47156CB00008B/2950